2-7

Dear Parents and Educators,

Welcome to Penguin Young Readers! As parents and educators, you know that each child develops at his or her own pace—in terms of speech, critical thinking, and, of course, reading. Penguin Young Readers recognizes this fact. As a result, each Penguin Young Readers book is assigned a traditional easy-to-read level (1–4) as well as a Guided Reading Level (A–P). Both of these systems will help you choose the right book for your child. Please refer to the back of each book for specific leveling information. Penguin Young Readers features esteemed authors and illustrators, stories about favorite characters, fascinating nonfiction, and more!

Annie™

LEVEL **3**

GUIDED READING LEVEL **L**

This book is perfect for a **Transitional Reader** who:
• can read multisyllable and compound words;
• can read words with prefixes and suffixes;
• is able to identify story elements (beginning, middle, end, plot, setting, characters, problem, solution); and
• can understand different points of view.

Here are some **activities** you can do during and after reading this book:
• Problem/Solution: The problem in this story is that Annie does not know where her parents are. Many years ago, they left her in an orphanage. Discuss the solution to this problem. Does Annie find her parents? Is she able to leave the orphanage?
• Venn Diagram: In this story, Miss Hannigan and Mr. Warbucks each take care of Annie. Think about how the two are alike and how they are different. On a separate piece of paper, draw a Venn diagram—two circles which overlap. Label one circle *Miss Hannigan* and the other *Mr. Warbucks*. Write the traits that are specific to each person in the parts of the circles that don't touch. Write the traits they share in the space where the circles overlap.

Remember, sharing the love of reading with a child is the best gift you can give!

—Bonnie Bader, EdM
  Penguin Young Readers program

*Penguin Young Readers are leveled by independent reviewers applying the standards developed by Irene Fountas and Gay Su Pinnell in *Matching Books to Readers: Using Leveled Books in Guided Reading*, Heinemann, 1999.

PENGUIN YOUNG READERS
Published by the Penguin Group
Penguin Group (USA) LLC, 375 Hudson Street, New York, New York 10014, USA

USA | Canada | UK | Ireland | Australia | New Zealand | India | South Africa | China

penguin.com
A Penguin Random House Company

ANNIE, ANNIE: THE MUSICAL & LITTLE ORPHAN ANNIE ®, ™ & © 2015 Tribune Content Agency,
LLC. All rights reserved. Published by Penguin Young Readers, an imprint of Penguin Group (USA) LLC,
345 Hudson Street, New York, New York 10014. Manufactured in China.

Library of Congress Control Number: 2014040479

ISBN 978-0-448-48223-1 (pbk)   10 9 8 7 6 5 4 3 2 1
ISBN 978-0-448-48224-8 (hc)   10 9 8 7 6 5 4 3 2 1

LEVEL 3

PENGUIN YOUNG READERS

TRANSITIONAL READER

Annie™

based on the original story by Thomas Meehan
adapted by Bonnie Bader
illustrated by Katie Kath

Penguin Young Readers
An Imprint of Penguin Group (USA) LLC

Annie was a little girl with curly
red hair. She did not have a mother
or a father.

She lived with other girls who did not have parents. They were called orphans (say: OR-funs). The orphans lived in a house with Miss Hannigan.

Miss Hannigan was very mean.
She made the girls work hard. They
had to scrub the floors. They had to
clean and clean and clean.

Annie did not like all the hard
work. She missed her real parents.
Annie had half a locket from her
parents. And she had a note that
said they would be back to get her
soon. She was sure her real parents
would come back to get her one day.

But it had been 11 years. And
Annie's parents had not come
to get her.

So she decided to go find them.

One day, a man came to pick up the laundry. Annie climbed inside the bag and hid. The man went outside. He put the bag in the back of his truck and drove away.

Annie was free!

Later, Annie climbed out of the
bag and out of the truck.

On the street, Annie found a dog.

"Oh, poor boy," Annie said to the
dog. He didn't have a home, either.

Suddenly, a policeman came
up to Annie. Annie knew that the
policeman was after the animal.

"Isn't that dog a stray?" he asked.

"Oh no, he is my dog," Annie said.

"So what is his name?"
the policeman asked.

"His name is Sandy," Annie said.

The policeman did not believe
that the dog was really hers.

"Let's see if he answers to his
name," the policeman said.

Annie was scared.

"Sandy!" she called.

The dog came running! The
policeman let Annie keep the dog.
Annie now had a dog and a friend.

But then Sandy ran away. And
another policeman caught Annie.
She was taken back to
Miss Hannigan.

Miss Hannigan was angry that Annie had run away. She yelled and yelled and yelled at Annie.

But then she stopped. Someone
was at the door.

It was a woman named Grace.
A rich man named Mr. Warbucks
had sent her. He wanted an orphan
to spend Christmas with him. And
Grace picked Annie!

Annie said good-bye to the other orphans.

Grace took Annie to Mr.
Warbucks's house. It was big and
beautiful.

"Annie, what do you want to do
first?" Grace asked.

"The floors," Annie said.

"You won't have to do any
cleaning while you are here," Grace
said.

"I won't?" Annie said.

"You are our guest," Grace said.

Mr. Warbucks came home. Annie was happy to meet him. He told Grace to take Annie to the movies.

Annie was sad. She wanted Mr. Warbucks to come, too.

"I'm afraid that I will be far too busy tonight," he told Annie.

But Annie would not take no for an answer.

At last, Mr. Warbucks agreed to go.

And they all had a wonderful
time! Soon, Annie and Mr. Warbucks
were going everywhere together.

Mr. Warbucks wanted Annie to live with him for good. He bought Annie a present.

"It's a silver locket," he said. "I saw that old, broken one you always wear. And I said to myself that I would get you a nice new locket."

Mr. Warbucks tried to take off
Annie's old locket.

"No, please don't make me take
my locket off!" Annie cried. She told
Mr. Warbucks that the locket was
from her parents. And she told him
that they were coming back for her.

"I'll find your parents for you,"
Mr. Warbucks said.

Mr. Warbucks and Annie went to the radio station. They said that Mr. Warbucks would pay a lot of money if Annie's parents were found.

Back at Miss Hannigan's house,
the orphans heard Annie on the
radio. Miss Hannigan heard the
news, too.

Just then, two people came into Miss Hannigan's house.

"Are you the lady who runs this place?" the man asked.

"Yes," Miss Hannigan said.

"We had to leave our baby here," the man said.

"Our little girl, Annie," the woman said.

"You are Annie's parents?" Miss Hannigan asked.

Then the man shouted, "I got you, sis!" It was Miss Hannigan's brother, Rooster, and his friend Lily.

They had a plan to trick Mr. Warbucks. They wanted Mr. Warbucks to think they were Annie's parents. Then they would get the money. They did not care what happened to Annie.

A lot of people said they were Annie's parents. But they were all fakes. Grace told Annie that all the people wanted was the money.

"You did your best," Annie told Mr. Warbucks. "If you can't find them, nobody can."

Mr. Warbucks knew he loved Annie.

"Annie, I want to adopt you," Mr. Warbucks said.

"If I can't have my real mother and father, there's no one in the world I'd rather have for a father than you," Annie said.

Mr. Warbucks had a big party on Christmas Eve. He was happy that he and Annie were together at last.

During the party, Rooster and Lily came in. They were dressed up as Annie's parents. They had a paper that said that Annie was their child. And they had the other half of Annie's locket. It was a perfect fit. Annie's parents were found!

Rooster wanted to take Annie
right away.

"What about the money?" Mr.
Warbucks asked.

"Money?" Rooster said. "We don't
have much, but we can give you
some."

Mr. Warbucks shook his head. He told Rooster and Lily that he was giving them money. Rooster and Lily said they did not want the money. But they were lying.

"Can Annie stay here until the morning?" Mr. Warbucks asked. "Then you can come back to pick up Annie and the money."

Rooster and Lily really wanted the money. But they said it was okay, and they left.

Mr. Warbucks wanted to get back to the party.

"We have just had the best news," he said. "Annie has found her mother and father."

But Annie was not happy.

She ran upstairs.

In the morning, Annie was ready to leave. She tried to put a smile on her face. Yet she still was not happy. She did not want to leave Mr. Warbucks.

Then Mr. Warbucks told her he had some news.

Annie's parents had been found.
She did not understand. Her
parents were already found.

Mr. Warbucks told Annie that the
people who had come were fakes.

"Annie, your mother and father
died a long time ago," he said.

"So, I am an orphan, after all," Annie said.

Annie knew that her real parents had loved her. And she knew that if they were still alive, they would have come back.

Now, Mr. Warbucks could become Annie's father. But first, they had to find out who the fake parents were.

Mr. Warbucks found out the truth. Rooster and Lily had faked the papers. And Miss Hannigan had told them about the locket. They were all sent to jail.

But what about the other orphans?

Mr. Warbucks said they could all live at his house. Annie was so happy!

Mr. Warbucks had one more
surprise.

"Sandy!"

Home at last!